Bettina Muenster

The little women

A Short Story

TWENTYSIX

A brand of Books on Demand GmbH

Production and Publishing:
BoD – Books on Demand, Norderstedt

ISBN 978-3-74078-616-8

Bibliographic information of the German National
Library: The German National Library lists this publication in
the German National Bibliography; detailed bibliographic data
are available on the Internet via dnb.dnb.de.

Bettina Muenster has been writing poems, short stories and novels since the age of thirteen.
The author is a member of the Independent Writer's Association in Germany.
After several self-publishing publications, she published her novel "The Curse of the Siren" in the Droemer Knaur Group in 2016. Further publications followed.
Bettina Muenster lives with her family in her adopted home of Hanover and is constantly writing new stories.

Up-to-date information on her projects can be found at:
https://bettinamuenster.wordpress.com

© 2022 Bettina Münster
Cover-Illustration: © Mimi Jamora
Book jacket: © Bettina Muenster
Translation into English © Bettina Muenster

IT was a warm summer evening. The sun had already put on its orange-red night dress to sink behind the horizon in peace and quiet. George sat in front of his cottage on the old, blue lacquered wooden bench and enjoyed the fresh bean stew he had cooked for dinner.

He liked to be alone. Only sometimes, in very beautiful, sad or lonely moments, did he long for a woman to share the whims of life with.

George was neither attractive, nor did he have much money. Only the small, whitewashed house by the sea and his fishing boat he called his own. At the age of forty, it would have been time to start a family. But the loneliness of his existence was not exactly inviting to women. And George had long since resigned himself to going through life alone.

When he had eaten his stew and brought the plate back to the cosy kitchen where the scent of onions and cooked vegetables still hung, he spontaneously decided to go up to the attic. There were the photo albums of his family, which he hadn't touched for many years. Since he was the only child of his parents who had died early, the photos showed only his childhood, only the family idyll of three.

George was a little melancholic that evening and wanted to sit down on the bench in front of the house with a glass of wine and the albums, enjoy dusk and reminisce.

He fetched his ladder, then pushed the flap in the ceiling upwards with effort and climbed up into the tiny, dark chamber.

It smelled musty. The coastal wind whistled slightly through the roof beams, as if to sing a secret melody intended only for George.

Slightly bent over, because he was too tall to be able to stand upright under the ridge of the roof, he purposefully walked towards the corner where he kept the memorabilia.

He was about to open the big box with the albums when suddenly something red shone towards him! Puzzled, he paused.

Hadn't something moved there? Right there in the corner, behind the box with his mother's garden tools?

Astonished, he came closer, pulled back the wooden box a little bit - and was deeply frightened: in front of him stood a tiny creature with fiery red hair and stared anxiously at him with wide-open eyes!

George could hardly believe what he saw. He stretched out his hand to reach for the little creature and see if it was real. But it ran away quickly! You could barely recognize the black-and-white striped socks and the red, pointed boots before it had run around a shelf and disappeared.

"That's not possible!"

The fisherman knelt down, carefully reached behind the old wooden shelf with one hand and closed his fingers around something soft and warm. Slowly he pulled it out.

"Let me go! How dare you! Let me go right away!"

A woman just as big as a finger is long, with fiery red hair, light green trousers, an equally green blouse and shiny red boots, hang, wildly struggling with her little legs, between his fingers.

George held her a little closer to his face. Apart from her size, the little woman looked normal. Only the auricles were a little pointed, as was her nose.

"Who are you? And what are you doing in my attic? How do you get here?"

"Hey! Let go of my sister immediately!", it suddenly shouted from the corner. George looked again at the shelf behind which he had brought out the little woman and saw that there was a second one standing there, with arms angrily akimbo! Now they came crawling out everywhere until the fisherman had nine little women standing in front of him, all with fiery red long hair and the same clothes. The tenth wriggled in his hand.

"What are you doing here?"

Meanwhile, the woman between his fingers was impatiently boxing his index finger, without George really feeling it. He also perceived the fact that she once bit him vigorously as a vague pinch.

"Well, what do you think! We live here! What do you want from us?"

George began to laugh quietly and sat down on the floor. He was careful not to accidentally sit on one of the little women.

"I live here, too! This is *my* attic, and it belongs to *my* house. How did you get in here? And what is your name anyway?"

The woman in his hand spoke up again: "My name is Emma. And we all crawled in under the back door a few years ago. You have a pretty big hole in there, do you know that?"

George thought for a moment. "Oh, you mean the knothole that's at the bottom of the door. Yes, that's right, it's big enough for you!"

Emma grinned. "Big enough? It's like an open door! For mice, too, by the way."

"So that's where they come from! Thanks for the tip, little Emma. But what are you doing up here? And why are you so small?"

Now, finally, he dropped the woman in his hand on the floor, whereupon she quickly ran back to her sisters. Another of the red-haired creatures stepped forward.

"We belong to the people of little women. We live together in groups in secrecy, so that you humans do not find and kill us."

Frightened, the fisherman looked at her. "But why should we kill you?"

"Well, you may not kill us, but lock us in cages like animals! Don't shake your head, we've seen it often enough!"

George stood up. "People sometimes do strange things when they are dealing with beings they don't know. We always want to control, explore and dominate everything. I'm afraid that's in most of us. But I regard it differently."

One of the women looked at him suspiciously. "Oh, and how do *you* see it then?"

George kindly smiled at her. "And your name is ...?"

"Linda. And this is my twin sister Sophie."

The man looked from one to the other and then laughed again. "Yes, that's right, you look exactly the same.
Look, it's not very homely up here. It is cold, humid and the wind whistles through the beams. In addition, it doesn't smell particularly pleasant. Why don't you come along and live in my kitchen? If you promise not to mess up, we will certainly find a place where you can make yourself comfortable."

The beings of the little people looked at their landlord in surprise, and for a moment there was complete silence. Then they threw their legs in the air with joy and cheered and danced together exuberantly! No one had ever been so kind to them!

It didn't take long for them to pack up their stuff and pull it out from behind the shelf. When George had put aside some boxes and old books, the whole world of the little women was revealed to him: in a cavity in the wall, they had created their own home. It almost looked like a doll's house!

"In the kitchen we find a place that is just as beautiful. Promised."

He packed all their things in a box and then lifted one woman after another into it. After making sure they held on well, he carefully brought them down, placed the box on the kitchen floor, and helped the women climb out again. It took less than an hour for the industrious little creatures to store their clothes, tiny dishes, blankets, pillows and many other little things in a spacious corner in George's cleaning chamber. It was only separated from the kitchen by a colorful curtain and offered enough space inside for the small people to set up. In addition, it was much drier and warmer here than up in the attic.

Then George wished the little red-haired creatures a good night and went to sleep. Before he closed his eyes, he wondered what miraculous coincidence had brought him these strange women, and how nice it was that he would now have company.

In the days that followed, time flew by. Sometimes George saw and heard nothing from his roommates for a whole day. On other occasions he came home and found them on the kitchen sideboard, where they had sat down comfortably and tied tiny bouquets of herbs or braided wreaths from grass. He never noticed how they got there or back again. But he didn't care either. They lived patiently and quietly side by side and rejoiced when they saw each other.

Then, one evening, as the fisherman sat at his table and ate bread with cheese, sipping a glass of wine and looking out of the window lost in thought, he suddenly felt that he was not alone. It took quite a while until he saw the little woman who had crawled shyly behind a table leg and looked up at him.

"Hello! Do we already know each other?"

She shook her head, played shyly with a long, curly strand, and asked: "Would you lift me up to the table? Maybe we can talk a little."

The fisherman did not allow himself to be asked twice. He liked conversations, and he had never spoken to a small woman in private. So he carefully picked her up and put her on the table, where she sat down on the handle of his bread knife.

"What are you eating there?"

George smiled and offered her a piece of cheese, which she gratefully accepted. But her expression spoke volumes when she bit into it, and so he laughingly gave her the tip of a handkerchief into which she spat the cheese.

"Excuse me, but this tastes really terrible. What is that?"

"This is cheese. It is made from the milk of goats. Would you rather try a little bread?"

The little woman gratefully declined and watched George quietly dinner for a while until he resumed their conversation: "Tell me a little bit about yourself and your people. I've never seen such small beings as you!"

"My name is Tina, and my sisters and I ... move every few years. But we haven't lived as beautiful as here for a long time!"

"Does there also exist a people of little men?"

She blushed and looked away embarrassed. "Yes, but we ... do not live together. Never. We only meet the little men ... on special occasions."

George could feel that the little woman was uncomfortable talking about it and quickly changed the subject.

"And why do you move every few years? You could stay where you are if you like it there. As long as no one discovers you."

"Yes, but ..." Again, a slight redness rose in Tina's face. She nervously crossed her fingers into each other. Now George became really curious and let his bitten piece of bread sink back onto the plate. He drank a sip of wine before he asked: "But what? Well, come on, Tina. Now tell me everything. Something is on your mind, isn't it?"

The little woman nodded and finally began to tell falteringly what made her people so unique: "You know, sometimes we are discovered and chased away. But there is one special thing ... well... When a man ... a human man, kisses us, we become human women."

George looked at her in amazement and almost choked on the cheese he had just bitten off. "You become human women? Normal size?"

Tina nodded.

"And now you want me to kiss you all so that you can live normally?"

"No! No, that's not how it works. We have laws."

Researching, he looked at the woman who was apparently sitting there so innocently on his knife.

"Tina ... what are you going to tell me?"

"If you kiss one of us, the other women have to leave the house. And the kissed one stays with you forever. This is an old law of our people."

"Aha."

For quite a while there was silence in the small kitchen. George tried to process what the woman with the fiery red hair had just told him. Then he slowly realized that *she* was the one who wanted to be kissed. But he was immediately sure that he *didn't* want that. How obviously calculating she had entrusted him with the secret of her people repelled and angered him.

"Tina, I can't just do that. I don't know you at all! If I have a woman by my side forever, then I want to make sure that she is the right one for me. In addition... what do your sisters say?"

She looked embarrassed to the ground. "They don't know I'm with you."

"Hm. So you secretly sneaked up on me. And you wouldn't mind if they left?"

She got up and guiltily rubbed her pointed nose. "Yes, of course! After all, they are my sisters. But I have always dreamed of being a human woman. Even if that means to become mortal."

George stared at her and was finally on the verge of losing his composure.

"You are *immortal?*"

"Yes. But... Well... I'll probably go back now. Perhaps... maybe you'll give me the chance to get to know each other better?"

George half-heartedly shrugged his shoulders and watched as Tina, elastic as an acrobat, jumped off the table and landed clean.

"We'll see. We'll see."

There was silence in the storage room. Tina lay on her fluffy camp of old cloths and stared into the darkness. It went differently than planned. Perhaps she had been too naïve. She knew for sure that she was the most beautiful of all the little women. And yet the fisherman had not wanted to kiss her. He had to be a little simple-minded.
Everyone would be happy to get Tina as their wife! And yet she was still one of the small people. Despite all efforts.

Suddenly, she started. Her sisters came up to her and stopped next to her bed, one by one. And they looked angry!

"Tina! You actually dared and went to him!"

Frightened, the woman sat up and immediately went on the attack. "That is my right! Each of you would have done the same!"

Emma built up in front of her and sparkled at her with angry, green eyes.

"We took a vow when we moved into this house! You remember it! We swore to ourselves that we all want to stick together and stay here! That we do not have to lose one more sister to the human people and don't need to move on! Why did you break the vow?"

Outraged, Tina now stood up and defiantly crossed her arms in front of her chest. "I didn't break the vow! George didn't kiss me! He will not jeopardize our vow!"

Emma came one step closer and said dangerously quietly: "I heard you. He didn't want to kiss you because he doesn't know you. But you asked him to give you a chance. A chance to get to know each other. You want him. Admit it!"

Caught, Tina stared at her sisters and turned red hot. With a triumphant laugh, Agatha, another of the little women, now entered the circle of the quarrelsome.

"I'll tell you what! Tina has broken the vow, so it is obsolete! The kiss must come from George, *he* must want it! You know what that means: from now on, each of us is allowed to woo him! Which means in plain language: nine of us will have to leave this house! It is up to each of us to make sure that she is not! And for my part, I don't want to move again!

Tina, however, I tell you one thing, and I believe that we all agree on this: if you are among those who must move on, you will be banished! The escape into human existence is more important to you than the cohesion with your sisters. So you are a danger to the community! As soon as we leave this house, you are on your own!"

With this, the nine sisters turned away from Tina and left her to her fate. The hunt for the kiss of the man was opened. From now on, as so often in the past, the ten of the people of the little women were competitors.

Only one woman was deeply frightened by her sisters' hunting instincts: Anna, the youngest and quietest of them. In her one hundred and fifty years of life, she had already moved many times, been expelled from houses and moved into new domiciles. And every time one of her sisters fell in love and courted the chosen one, she suffered hellish torments. Anna did not have the soul of a vagabond. She dreamed of settling, staying in one place and living there with her sisters. She had never wanted anything else.

When they had taken the swearing not to be kissed by a man when they moved into the fisherman's house, a stone had fallen from her heart. Anna, in her infinite naivety, had believed that she had finally found the place for life.

Her heart became heavy at the sight of the other women who went back to their own beds with grim faces, each determined to win the fisherman's heart for herself. As always, when disaster threatened, she withdrew into herself and distanced from the others.

Secretly, so that her sisters wouldn't notice, she already began to pack her things.

Agatha was the first to venture a day later. She tried to charm George with her beautiful big eyes, but he found her overly confident nature repulsive and turned her down.

When she left, deep in thought, he went out fishing with his boat. In the evening he returned tired and with several large fishes over his shoulder. In the kitchen he was already expected by Emma. He found her standing on the sideboard.

"I made you something to eat!", she shouted proudly, and presented him with a bowl of pudding that was enormously large by her standards.

When George took the bowl in his hands, it quickly became clear that it was no bigger than a nutshell for him. Emma blushed and wanted to retire, but he stopped her: "Please wait. Thank you. You've made an effort with it, and I'm sure I'll enjoy the pudding."

'*If I manage to sip it out of this tiny bowl*', he thought to himself, but only smiled gratefully and looked after the woman who ran back into the chamber with an embarrassed expression on her face.

One after the other, nearly all of the little women made their appearance to him, until George almost regretted having let them into his kitchen. In the attic, he would never have noticed anything about them, and everyone could have led their own existence!

When he came out of the church on Sunday, he saw all ten little women standing in the door to the storeroom.

"Have you been waiting for me?" Instead of getting an answer, ten fiery red hair scoops nodded eagerly to him.

"So nice of you. I'm going to make a roast pork now. Do you like that? With lots of vegetables and delicious potatoes? In addition, I will bake a cake later this afternoon."

The little women laughed and clapped their hands with joy.

"We love roasts and cakes!"

After lunch, George sat at his table full and satisfied and watched the women sitting cross-legged on the tabletop talking and weaving baskets of grass.

Suddenly, he noticed that one little woman hadn't said anything yet. Also, George couldn't remember ever consciously having noticed this sister before.

She had been very quiet while eating and had fully concentrated on the enjoyment of the meal.

Suddenly, his curiosity was aroused. All the other women tried to charm him. Why did she hold back so much? He carefully stroked her upper arm with a finger to draw her attention to himself. The little woman was so frightened that she almost knocked over her plate, which she was still balancing on her knees.

"Excuse me, I didn't want to scare you. You're so quiet all the time. What is your name?"

"Anna."

Shyly, she looked at him from below, with her big button eyes catching his breath. As if spellbound, he stared at her.

"Your eyes ... They're blue."

Anna nodded and quickly lowered her gaze again.

"I'm the only one of us with blue eyes. Apparently, something went wrong with me."

George angrily shook his head. "Something went wrong? Just because you have a different eye color than everyone else? Nobody has ever told you that it makes you special, right?"

"Oh, leave her. Anna never says a word. She probably doesn't have much to say. She always reads books and so. What kind of cake are you baking right away?"

Agatha had stood up and clumsily pushed herself into the foreground. Suddenly, George realized how repellent her behavior was.

"Agatha, I'm talking right now."

Turning to Anna again, he asked: "Would you like to help me bake?"

George could see her little heart pounding violently under the green blouse.

"*I* should help you?" With trembling fingers, she stroked a stray strand of hair behind her right ear.

"Yes, if you like. Unless you don't like to bake."

A glance into her bright blue eyes was enough for him to know that he had won.

And so he sent the other nine sisters out into the garden to collect herbs, even if they were anything but enthusiastic about it. He wanted to be alone with Anna.

"But I can also collect herbs ..." George interrupted her kindly: "No, I want you to keep me company."

He lifted her off the table and placed her on the kitchen sideboard, where he lined up all the baking ingredients in front of her one after the other.

"How come I haven't met you yet?"

Anna had sat down on the package with butter and dangled indecisively with her legs.

"I don't know. I am very much with my sisters."

He softly laughed. "Yes, that must be the case. Otherwise I would certainly have noticed you. That being said: you're the only little woman who hasn't tried to make me give away a kiss yet."

Overwhelmed by so much directness, Anna blushed and stopped dangling her legs. Very quietly she said: "You know our law now. I have... I'm afraid of it."

George's exploratory gaze pierced her. "You don't want to be transformed?"

Uncertainly, she once again brushed a strand of hair from her face.

"No, I don't mean that. But... I am loyal to my sisters. I have nobody else in the world except of them. And I don't want to be to blame if they must leave. Because I, myself, am terribly afraid of having to leave this house again. I had hoped to finally arrive here. But I hope so every time. And then I have to say goodbye again."

It took a few thoughtful minutes for George to put eggs and flour in the bowl and pour some milk on the mixture until he understood the full extent of her words. Anna was an incredibly sensitive person. She was loyal and first thought of the group, her family.

"Anna, please look at me."

The little woman lifted her gaze, and he looked at her for a long time, looked in these blue ponds that radiated so much magic and vulnerability.

"Dear Anna, don't you want to stay with me?"

She winced and quickly got up from the butter pack. George smiled tenderly: she had melted a small hollow into the butter with her body heat.

"I really have to go now and help my sisters. Otherwise they will get angry that I have been here with you for so long."

Before he had a chance to hold her back, she had jumped off the sideboard and walked out the kitchen door.

But the little woman named Anna wouldn't leave George's head. Not when he put the cake into the oven, nor when he sat on his bench in front of the house in the evening and put on his pipe.

When the night had passed over his house, he tiptoed into the kitchen, made light, went to the storeroom and looked around the realm of the little women until he discovered Anna. She had made her bed in a small wooden soap dish that had once belonged to George's mother.

He knew it was selfish, but the fisherman had fallen in love for the first time in his life, which he never thought possible. He wanted to share his life with this woman.

And so he lifted up the bowl with Anna sleeping firmly in it, carefully placed it in the middle of his kitchen floor and bent over the deeply and evenly breathing being.

One last time he looked at the tiny, dense eyelashes, the snub nose and the pointed ear cups, gently stroked over them with the top of his index finger. Then he bent down and kissed Anna gently on the mouth.

The End

https://bettinamuenster.wordpress.com

www.textzirkus.com